Maxkii-Wiixcheew

(The Story of Red Wolfe)

Maxkii-Wiixcheew
(The Story of Red Wolfe)

B Shawn Clark

Englewood, Florida USA

Copyright 2025 B Shawn Clark

Maxkii-Wiixcheew (*The Story of Red Wolfe*) is a work of speculative historical fiction. While based on actual events taking place in 1663 (sometimes referred to as the 2nd Esopus "War") and historical figures, including Abraham DuBois (the author's ancestor) references to historical events, real people, or real places are used fictitiously. Resemblances in this work to real-life people or historical events should not be regarded as factual, especially in the case of indigenous peoples living in the Hudson River such as the Esopus. Any opinions expressed in this novel are those of the characters and should not be confused with those of the author - nor anyone else.

ISBN: 978-1-7343083-9-6 (this paperback)

ISBN: 979-8-9879174-0-4 (eBook)

Front and back cover artwork by SRB McKenzie.

Book design by First Run Books.

Printed by IngramSpark, in the U.S. (and elsewhere).

First "printing" eBook edition 2023. This edition: 2025.

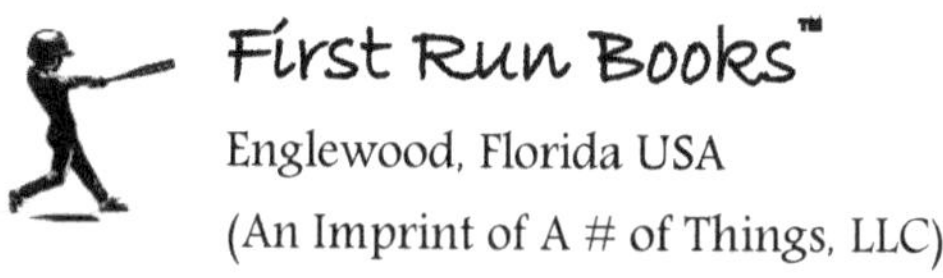
First Run Books™
Englewood, Florida USA
(An Imprint of A # of Things, LLC)

www.maxkii-wiixcheew.com

Dedication

Anushiik Kiisheelumukweengw
Eelu Miiluyan Chloe:
Pasusuw wiixcheew.
Pasusuw musuchee.

(To Chloe. Half wolf. Half not.)

Lunaape Language Acknowledgement

Languages spoken by different people from different parts of the world are a central theme of this book, starting with the title character. His name in the ancient language known as Lunaape combines the word for red (maxkii) with the word for wolf (wiixcheew) in a hyphenated proper noun intended to convey how this fictional character's spirit name may have been pronounced in 1663.

As you can see the translation of Maxkii-Wiixcheew that appears in the subtitle ("Red Wolfe") is not a literal translation of the two words that when combined yields the character's spirit name, nor is it a misspelling of the English word for "wolf." Readers will have to wait until they reach the final chapter of the book to find clues as to why this is so.

Lunaape is the term used by the few remaining speakers of it (now living primarily in a community near Ontario, Canada) to identify the language likely spoken by the Munsee (Delaware) people known as the Esopus.

While by no means proficient, the author gained enough knowledge of the Lunaape language from his Munsee teacher to be able to bring a few words of this endangered language to life in this book.

This includes the dedication (derived from portions of a Lunaape prayer), the chapter numbers (one through ten in English) and the name of the title character that appears on the cover and throughout the pages of this book.

The author participated in classes to learn the Lunaape language through a program sponsored by Historic Huguenot Street in New Paltz, New York, where his ancestor, Abraham DuBois is buried.

While doing research for this book, he discovered (through a local historian) that Abraham had learned to speak Lunaape during his time living among the Esopus.

Abraham (and other Huguenots) also most likely spoke primarily a very old version of French and no doubt a fair amount of Dutch. Ironically enough, although written in English, this book contains dialogue from characters that at the time this story took place did not speak that language (except by the English-speaking soldiers who make a brief appearance at the end of the book).

Only through the willing suspension of disbelief can readers enjoy this book, knowing that the words spoken by its characters could not possibly have been spoken in the English language we know today. Those words as originally spoken, now nearing the point of extinction, are all the more important to hear. They speak to us through the ages in halting refrains, having been all but wrung out of the First Nation peoples by those who came after.

But there are still some who are dedicated to awakening these sleeping words.

It is in that spirit, and with utmost honorable respect that the few words of Lunaape that grace the pages of this book are humbly presented to its readers.

For more information about the Lunaape language and efforts underway to preserve it, please visit the following page on this book's webpage devoted to that subject:

http://www.maxkii-wiixcheew.com/lunaape.html

Pronunciation of basic words in Lunaape are also presented on that webpage.

Please be aware that the United Nations in 2022 estimated that, worldwide, an indigenous language disappears every 2 weeks. Consequently, there is an urgent need for those people interested in preserving languages at risk – both indigenous and non-indigenous people alike – to show interest in Languages such as Lunaape.

Even so, non-indigenous people (such as the author) must proceed with caution and respect for these languages, regarded as sacred by the communities from which they originated, keeping in mind that, despite a well-grounded basis to distrust the Huguenots in 1663, speakers of Lunaape chose to share their language with Abraham DuBois.

Preface

This book is a work of historical fiction. Action taking place in the book is based on well-documented events described euphemistically as the Second Esopus "War" by the European invaders of Turtle Island, who in 1663 mercilessly carried out what can be fairly characterized as ethnic cleansing (if not genocide) of the Esopus community.

Needless to say the perpetrators of this massacre, such as Captain Marten Kregier (whose field notes are the main source material for what happened) do not describe themselves as mass murders. His account, along with those of a handful of others, do not present the facts objectively and certainly not from the point of view of the Esopus.

Kregier and the DuBois family are real historical figures. Other characters such as Maxkii-Wiixcheew and Standing Bear, are technically fictional but their existence does have some basis in reality. Who they were, what they said and what they did has to be imagined because there are no records documenting their point of view.

The existence of the couple from Marbletown appears to also be well-grounded in fact.

The primary resource relied upon for this book, both as to what happened in 1663, as well as what it likely would have been like to live among the Esopus, can be found in *The Munsee Indians, A History*, by Robert S. Grumet (2009).

Table of Contents

NGWUTA - The God of Abraham

In the beginning the God of Abraham created all living things and a world where they would all live. Man was given dominion over all the other creatures of the world. These things were told to Abraham at a very early age.

Abraham himself was named for his brother, although he did not come to know this until many years later when he was a man. His brother was born before he was. His parents eventually explained to him that God had taken the first Abraham back shortly after he was born.

They gave Abraham his name.

Like most people Abraham does not remember many things about life on the farm in Germany where he spent the first three years of his life. But as far back as he can remember, his parents told him the story of Abraham in Genesis, the first book of the Bible, although he never did understand why they called it a "book." Wasn't the Bible itself a book? He didn't quite understand that but was too ashamed to ask why this was so.

He didn't want to seem ignorant about something as important as that. Or maybe he was just a little bit afraid to ask such a question out loud. His father was, after all, an imposing figure. The minister at the church was even more intimidating, especially when he was giving a sermon.

Abraham was too young at the time to understand most of what the minister was talking about when his parents took him to church. This was not because the minister was speaking French. They all spoke French in that part of Germany where Abraham was born and where his father Louis DuBois and mother Catherine had moved a few years before he was born.

They had to leave their beloved France because they were Huguenots. Huguenots were a special breed of people who were very passionate about their particular interpretation of the Bible, but that did not sit well with the Catholic Church.

Many of them were forced to leave France, which was becoming too dangerous for them if they wanted to believe what they thought the Bible taught them about how to live their lives. The place in Germany where Abraham's parents settled welcomed the ingenious – and industrious – Huguenots, even though they did not speak German, the native tongue of the place where they sought refuge.

Although he did not have many memories of life on the farm there in Germany, a few things must have made quite the impression on Abraham's young mind.

They became very vivid memories that stuck with him his entire life. One of them was when his little brother was born. He remembered that day when the minister and some other people came to the house. They were standing around his infant brother while the minister was reading from his Bible.

They were doing something to his little brother but Abraham was too little to see what they were doing, even when he stood on his tiptoes and tried to crane his neck to peer through the adults who were clustered tightly around where his little brother was lying, swaddled, on the top of an old wooden table.

"What are they doing to my brother?" he asked loud enough to be heard.

"Shhhhhh!" came the answer from no one in particular and from everyone.

Abraham could see the minister glaring at him through a crack in the crowd of people who must have parted like the great Sea of Galilee just enough for the minister to deliver that stern look. That is when Abraham finally caught a glimpse of his brother lying helpless on the table. He also saw the glint of light shining off something sharp the minister was holding in his hand.

The look of horror on his face was apparently palpable enough that his mother bent down to his eye level and smiled sweetly at him. "Your brother is being circumcised," she told him. "This is part of our traditions, as given to us by the Lord our God. You, too, were circumcised in the same way as Isaac."

"Isaac?" The expression of horror on Abraham's face had turned quizzical.

"That is the name we have given your brother," Louis said as he drew closer, towering over the boy. Abraham's mother stood up from her kneeling position and stepped back with a slight bow of her head. Louis took another step forward. He bent down slightly, his hands on his knees, drawing his face closer, engulfing the entire field of vision of the little boy. "Remember the Book of Genesis? God blessed Abraham with the miracle of a child. His name means 'laughter' because Abraham and Sarah, Isaac's mother, thought it was funny to think that they could have a child at their age. But true to His Word, God gave them Isaac."

"Isaac. My brother's name is *Isaac.*"

Louis stood up, smiling down at his little boy who grew an inch or two in that moment, at least in the eyes of his father. "Yes. Your brother is Isaac. He is named for one of the ancestors of the people who became known as the twelve tribes of Israel.

You, too, are named for another one of these ancestors, the first to whom God spoke. And now Isaac has become a part of our own tribe. He is your brother, and you are his keeper. You must watch over him as much as your mother and I will be watching over the both of you, to make sure you are safe."

Louis looked over at Catherine and smiled. She smiled back at him.

In the years to follow Abraham's parents did, indeed, bear many children, all of whom became members of the DuBois tribe. But in that moment there was just the four of them. Then a cry rang out from across the room, drawing their attention to the wooden table where the minister was standing over little Isaac.

This scene left an indelible imprint on the young mind and memory of little Abraham. So, too, did the time when his ox was born. A cow had just given birth to a calf. Abraham heard all about the new addition to their livestock the night before.

He was keenly interested in what he thought was a new addition to their tribe.

"What will we name him?" he asked. His father gave him a knowing look.

"We do not give names to the animals over which we have dominion," Louis told him. "They are not pets, and it is not wise to think of them as such."

"Why not?" Louis' expression became more serious as he leaned closer to his son, whose eyes widened. Catherine looked on, a look of concern on her face.

"You will learn the answer to that question in due time. But for now, we must neuter this new calf, who shall remain nameless."

"What does 'neuter' mean?" asked Abraham.

Louis glanced over at Catherine to gauge how well he was doing in explaining to such a young boy the harsh realities of farm life and the eventual fate to be suffered by the animals over which they believed they had been given dominion by God. Her expression had relaxed. She would have to remain content with leaving these matters to father and son.

"Neutering is like circumcision. Remember that? We just have to cut a little deeper than we do with infant boys. We have to do that while they are still young, before they grow into large bulls with very sharp horns. In the Bible, a man who lets his bull gore people can be punished very severely. So we must neuter them. It makes them more docile and easier to manage."

Louis looked over at Catherine for approval. She had a weak smile on her face.

"What your father is telling you is true," she said, turning to Abraham, "but there are some who say the Bible counsels against this practice, and neutered animals are forbidden to be offered as a gift to God." Louis started to frown. "But, as your father said, if the Bible teaches that we must circumcise our young, why can we not do something similar when it comes to our oxen?"

Abraham still did not understand all of these things but accepted the explanation that his parents gave to him. The next day he went out into the field where the new calf was lying down in the grass. His father and a group of men were knelt down, encircling the animal. The minister was not among them.

He heard a sharp cry from the calf that reminded him of that day Isaac was circumcised. His father rose from the assembled men. Blood covered his shirt and overalls.

He was holding something squishy and bloody in his hand.

Abraham's mouth fell open as he watched his father silently turn and walk towards the barn while the other men tended to the wounded bull calf, henceforth to be known as an ox.

Images of what Abraham had witnessed that day appeared in his mind many months later as he stood on the dock with his mother, holding the hand of little Isaac, who always wanted to stand up even though he could barely walk.

They looked down as the men were loading their livestock onto the ship that would carry them on an adventure to a new land. Abraham could swear that the little calf, now half grown into the very large ox he was to become, looked up at him.

Isaac waved to him.

NIISHA – Tribe of Wolves

Among the Esopus a man who would come to be known as Maxkii-Wiixcheew belonged to a clan that was known by the word meaning "wolf" in the language then spoken by the Munsee, a nation of peoples who had lived in the Hudson River Valley for thousands of years before the white man came. But the clan to which Maxkii-Wiixcheew belonged is not how he got his name. The legend among his people was that he was given his name by a medicine man of his tribe who had interpreted what had happened to Maxkii-Wiixcheew after he had returned from the forest from a vision quest.

Maxkii-Wiixcheew was but a little boy when the meaning of his vision quest – and his name – was revealed to him. He was a little bit older than Abraham was when Abraham was told the meaning of his name on the occasion of his brother's circumcision. The difference in how each of these two boys learned the secret of their names was as far and wide as the ocean that separated them from one another.

As with all of the members of the clan known as Wolf, when his time had come, the boy later known as Maxkii-Wiixcheew was led into the place where the village elders held their council.

He could not remember all of the wisdom that was imparted to him by the elders that morning, but he did remember being led into the forest afterwards to embark upon his vision quest. His memory of wandering into the forest was as hazy as his mind had been at the time. He felt queasy after breathing in the smoke of the shaman at their council. His head was swimming with words that they had spoken that he did not understand.

His stomach began to growl at him in protest, beseeching him for an answer to his hunger and thirst.

"Hush, I must be still and listen for a sign as the wise men told us would come to us. After that, then we can have a feast to our heart's content!"

But his stomach at first did not seem to be listening very well to his words. Then he realized that it was not his stomach that was growling at him. He peered into a thicket and saw a pair of red ambers returning his stare.

Instinctively he crouched, reaching for the handle of the sharpened stone tucked into the waistband of his deerskin breechcloth. It was the only tool he was allowed to bring with him on this vision quest. Now it was to be his only weapon.

The she-wolf lunged for him, her jaw open and fangs exposed, aiming for the veins on the little boy's neck. He screamed as he was toppled over by the force of fur and muscle and fangs that had been flung at him with such fury.

He fell backwards, landing hard, the beast prone on top of him. His eyes were clenched tightly shut. He waited for the final blow and the flow of that warm liquid he felt spreading on his chest to turn into a torrent.

He asked the Great Spirit to commend him to that place where small boys slain by their fellow creatures of the forest go when their time has come and they would no longer feel the earth beneath their feet.

After a few minutes of lying there, the she-wolf lying motionless on top of him, he heard what sounded like the cries of small pups coming from the thicket. He opened his eyes to behold the face and jaws of the she-wolf not more than five inches from his own. She had a look on her face that to him was one of shock and surprise. He pushed the dead carcass off of him, running his hand over the bright crimson moistness that covered his torso. He looked down at his bloody hand that had held his meager means of defense – one that had proved sturdy enough to save him from the ferocious onslaught of his assailant.

With a long pull that took most of the strength he had left, he retrieved his makeshift blade lodged under the breastbone and through the heart of the beast, no doubt impaling her through the force of her own weight when she pounced upon him. Then there was that sound again, coming from the thicket.

He turned towards the sound, his weapon and his body poised to continue the battle with any strength he could muster. But when the two cubs emerged from the thicket, he suddenly realized what he had done. The she-wolf was just protecting her young from the threat he unintentionally posed to them. They were like him, babes in the woods. But he had his mother, head of the Wolf Clan, to go home to.

They had no one.

The boy crumpled in a heap upon the forest floor.

He was sobbing uncontrollably, lathered in blood and sorrow for what he had done. Soon the moist protrusions from the mouths of the two babes raked what felt like grains of sand across his face and on his arm. Were they lapping up the blood for their morning meal or soothing him by drying the tears that had been running down his face?

He staggered to his feet and watched as the two cubs sniffed at the dead carcass of their mother, and then looked up at him, their heads cocked to one side. He turned and made his way back to the village to answer for his crimes.

Surely his vision quest had run its course, and the meaning of what had happened to him and, more importantly, why he was chosen to bear this burden would be revealed to him by the elders before they meted out the justice he deserved.

He looked back as he made his way down the trail towards the village. The cubs were following him. He stopped for a moment and stared at them. They stared back at him. He continued to walk. They continued to follow.

By the time he made it back to the village, the wolf blood smeared on his face and body was dried and hung caked on his skin. He must have been quite the sight as he approached the men sitting around the fire.

But they scarcely seemed to notice the frightful figure of the boy from the clan of the wolf now clothed in the life essence of his clan's namesake, emerging from the edge of the forest.

"I have done a terrible thing. I have killed the mother of two young wolf cubs who are now orphans. They are now at the mercy of the forest," the boy cried out.

"You mean those two?" the medicine man said, motioning to a spot behind the boy where the cubs had followed him into the clearing. The boy turned around to regard the two cubs. They were looking up at him, their heads again tilted to one side. They were as unsure about what would happen next as he was.

"Yes. They are the witnesses to my crime." The boy sat down with a thud next to the men. He was bone weary. His mind was reeling with thoughts and images of fang, blood and scratchy tongues on skin. He buried his head in his hands but was too exhausted for more tears to come yet again.

Then he felt the tell-tale raking of moist sand on his arms and his face. He opened his eyes, staring absently at the two cubs. Their heads, as usual, were tilted to one side.

"You have committed no offense against the ways of the forest, Maxkii-Wiixcheew. You have but learned your place among the other creatures that dwell in the land of the Great Spirit. Your place is a very important one within your clan and among your people. You have been given a vision that has spoken to you of a furious storm that approaches, threatening you and your people.

"You must prepare to protect us, and our ways, even from our own mothers and fathers, for the threat comes not only from the outside, but also from here," said the medicine man, thumping his hand hard against his breast.

"The storm that comes to take our people and our lives from us do not understand our ways, or the ways of the forest. They are men who have long forgotten that they are themselves among many creatures brought into this world by the Creator. They make slaves of their fellow creatures. They do not honor the Great Spirit that binds all living things together as one. They enslave the rest of the world and believe they are our masters, when they are themselves enslaved by their own ways.

"They thirst for the power over all living things, but their thirst can never be quenched because it is like a mirage in the distance. It is not real."

The boy now known in his tribe as Maxkii-Wiixcheew (Red Wolf) listened to these words. He did not understand all of them.

In time he would.

NXAH - Step the Ox

Abraham went out to the stable early most days. He was still quite young but his father thought him old enough to help tend to the oxen. His mother thought otherwise.

But Louis was the man of the house and was in charge of making decisions such as this.

Abraham was glad for it.

He was smart enough to know what could happen if an ox got out of hand, even before the lecture he received by that man with the big dent in his leg from being nearly gored to death. You had to be very firm with the oxen. They had to know who was in charge, even if the boy in charge brandishing a lean switch in his hand was but a mere pipsqueak as compared to the lumbering behemoth standing next to him. Not that Abraham ever actually swatted his ox. Goodness knows the poor thing had been pelted plenty enough by other people. He didn't need to be reminded who was in charge through brute force. The ox got the idea.

All Abraham had to do was wave the thing in the air to get his attention.

Sometimes Abraham let Isaac come with him when he went to feed their ox. He kept close watch over his brother to make sure he did not get crushed underfoot.

"Why do you call him 'Step'?" Isaac asked one day.

"What do you mean?"

"Isn't that his name?"

Abraham looked at his little brother, puzzled at the question. Then he realized what Isaac meant. One of the commands he had learned from the guy with the dented leg was "step up!" That was the signal for the ox to move forward. Isaac must have heard him pause between the words "step" and "up," thinking that he was calling out the name of the ox before asking him to raise his leg.

Abraham was about to correct his little brother's misimpression, but then he thought better of it. Once he told Isaac that the ox was not named "Step," the next question would have been, "Well, if his name isn't 'Step,' what is it?" Then he would have to explain that they did not give names to their animals, which would have then led to the inevitable question, "Why?" Aside from ushering in a series of never- ending one-word questions "Why?" that little kids like Isaac like to do, Abraham was keenly aware that he still did not know the answer to that question.

Why *didn't* they give names to their oxen?

"You are right, little man. His name is Step."

"Why?" came the quick retort.

"Because."

"Because *why*?"

"Because I said so, that's why. But don't try it on him. He doesn't listen to just anybody, you know. He likes to listen to me though. Plus, he likes the name, as far as I can tell. We are sort of like kin to one another. Of course, he is not like a brother to me, like you are but almost." Abraham smiled. His answer seemed to stop the "why" questions, for the moment at least. Isaac fell silent, lost in thought.

Abraham decided that calling the ox "Step" was not such a bad idea after all.

He was not exactly breaking the rules when he said, "Step, Up!"

His father would be none the wiser.

He did not realize it at the time, but oxen do tend to bond with their human handlers, one in particular. Even children can become regarded by an ox as their best friend, someone who they will listen to not only because they have to, but because they want to. An ox is much more powerful than the little boy telling them what to do. Yet they give up their power to the little munchkin waving that stick around. Maybe they are just trying to please the little tike. It is not so much a master-servant relationship as it is one born of misplaced affection.

In the case of Abraham and Step, the affection was anything but misplaced, even though the boy knew enough that Step was not to be thought of as a pet.

One day, Abraham was heading out to the fields to coax Step and the other animals back to the stable.

It was near dusk.

He kept his eyes to the ground so as to watch his own step. Isaac was following behind him. They heard the sound of gunfire. A single shot, off in the distance where they knew Step would be.

They raced towards the sound of the gun shot and saw their father. He was near the edge of the field, standing over the body of a young wolf.

"What happened? Is Step – I mean, are the oxen okay?" The little boy was out of breath, pushing the words out as best he could.

"The oxen are just fine and so is your father, in case you were wondering about that," Louis said. "There was a pack of wolves that were getting a little too close for comfort. They looked pretty hungry. But it's okay, I scared them off."

Isaac came running up and stopped short. He looked at the dead wolf and all the blood, and then at his father. His eyes started to well up with tears. He trudged over to where the body of the wolf was lying and sat down next to him, cradling the head of the young wolf in his arms, stroking his fur.

His father walked over and knelt down beside him, speaking softly. "I tried to scare them off, but they just didn't get the message. I had to shoot at them to get them to leave. I wasn't even intending to kill this one. Just a lucky shot, I guess."

He tapped young Isaac on the shoulder. His little boy looked up at him with a bewildered, yet calm expression on his face.

"Son, you must understand that these are wild creatures. They do not know the law of God. They only know the law of the wilderness. If he were alive now, this wild animal would just as soon eat you as look at you if given half a chance."

Isaac said nothing as his father stood up and headed in the direction of where the oxen and other cattle were grazing. He stopped and turned towards Abraham.

"Maybe you should take your brother back to the house. I'll take care of the animals including that one ox – let's see, what did you call him? – oh yeah, 'Step.'" He paused for a moment. "I thought I told you not to give names to the animals."

"Shall we bury this one?" Abraham asked, motioning towards the dead wolf. He decided not to try and explain the whole thing about how "Step" was not really the name of the ox, it was just a command.

"It will be dark soon. If you want to bury him, you better do it quick. And don't be surprised if his own pack of wolves digs up the body and makes a meal of him. He will probably be gone by morning. You and your brother can put some stones on his body or, better yet, drag it into the woods. Just make sure the other wolves are not still around and be sure to get him back before dark." He motioned with his head towards Isaac, who was now rocking back and forth, humming some sort of song under his breath. If you are out past dark, there will be hell to pay for all three of us. You know how your mother worries."

"C'mon, let's put some stones on him before we get in real trouble," Abraham said, gently stroking his brother's back. Isaac looked up at him and nodded.

They haphazardly piled stones on the carcass, keeping a wary eye out for any signs of wolves lurking in the bushes. They had a feeling someone was watching them, but they kept on working until it was nearly dark. When they thought they had a respectable enough barrow, they got ready to go back to the house.

"Wait, we should say something," Abraham said.

They both paused, solemnly clasping their hands in front of them like they did sometimes in church. "Let's see, here lies a brave wolf who was, was . . ."

"Wolfie," Isaac said softly. He looked over at his brother. "That is his name I gave him." Abraham decided not to correct his brother. They were not supposed to give names to animals.

He was beginning to understand why.

"Wolfie it is then. Here lies Wolfie, a brave creature of the forest who is no more, except in our hearts." Abraham touched his chest for emphasis.

So did Isaac.

The sky had grown dark, and a full moon rose up over the tree line. Then they heard wolves howling in the distance.

They made a run for it back to the house as fast as their little legs could carry them.

NEEWA - 13 Moons
on a Turtle's Back

How many moons did Maxkii-Wiixcheew watch cross the sky in the year that the White Man descended upon the villages of his people? He was not sure of the answer to that question, but he knew that it was in the season of the hunger, when he returned with a hunting party with much-needed food they were bringing back to his village.

They were greeted by a sight he would never forget.

Before them lie their ravaged homes, wailing and the sounds of the injured moaning rising up from the still smoldering fires that had been set to their village.

The initial shock was soon replaced by a smoldering of anger in the heart of Standing Bear, the leader of the hunting party, and the others who looked on.

"What happened?" Standing Bear asked the first person he saw as he rushed forward into the village, Maxkii-Wiixcheew and the others close behind. She was a younger woman sitting with an old man's head cradled in her lap, blood oozing from the wound in his forehead. She looked up, squinting at the towering brave.

"The White Devils came as if blown in by a terrible wind from the east. They killed my father," she said, looking down again at the old man in her lap. "They must have thought that he was not important enough to take him as a prisoner as they have in other villages. We have been told that they took 13 in all. My father told me just before he closed his eyes for the last time that the Whites must have taken one for each of the moons on the turtles' back."

During the raids the White Man had taken sachems, shamans and other leaders that they thought worthy enough to bring the tribes of the Esopus to their knees, including the medicine man who had interpreted Maxkii-Wiixcheew's visions and had given him his name. Maxkii-Wiixcheew now began to understand the prophecy that had been linked to his destiny – a destiny he still did not understand how to fulfill.

Standing Bear and the other braves gathered at what was left of the council fire in the village. They had spent the day repairing damage and sending out scouts into the forest and other nearby villages and campsites. Maxkii-Wiixcheew himself was sent out with an older brave. They crossed paths with an injured warrior who was able to follow the soldiers and horses of the Whites for some distance.

"They are heading back east with their death and their prisoners," he told them. "We must know what they want to make them return our people to us."

Back at the council fire the words of the injured warrior were repeated, as were those of others who told of the hostages that had been taken and the war the White Man was waging against the Esopus.

"We must respond in kind," Standing Bear said. "The Great White Father of the East will not return our people to us in exchange for wampum and even the land that they thirst to have as their own. That thirst will never be quenched except by the blood of our people spilled upon the earth."

"Then what do we do?" Maxkii-Wiixcheew heard himself ask. He was standing behind the men sitting at the council fire. Standing Bear peered out and over their heads in the direction of the young voice he heard through the smoke-filled night air.

"We must join with the other clans and tribes to take from the Whites what they have taken from us. Then they may listen to reason. We will take their women and hold them as ransom for the return of our men."

"Do the White Devils also regard women as the head of their clans?" another brave asked of Standing Bear.

"We do not fully understand the ways of the White Man," Standing Bear replied. "They have no honor. They do not honor the women of the Wolf, Turtle and Turkey Clans. They do not honor the creatures of the forest or even the land itself that they crave to have for themselves while our people starve.

"They have no honor in battle so we do not know that their men will surrender and go peacefully with us when we return the favor and attack their villages. We are already hearing from the other clans and tribes throughout our besieged land that we must retain our own honor and attack the White Man and take their women."

"What about their children?"

It was Maxkii-Wiixcheew again.

Standing Bear looked out into the darkness in Maxkii-Wiixcheew's direction. The stern look on his face softened almost imperceptibly, there in the glow of the flickering fire.

"Do not worry, my brother, whose wolves follow him like those of the clan that bears their name. We have honor that the White Man lacks. We will take the children as well as their mothers. They will become members of our own tribes and clans if they are not sent back in exchange for our own people."

Afterward, Maxkii-Wiixcheew approached Standing Bear.

"I hope I did not speak too much out of turn," he said.

Standing Bear laid his huge paw of a hand on the little boy's shoulder, the twin wolves eyeing him closely. "We have lost many leaders in these times," he said softly. You are blossoming now into a man who will take their place."

"Then I will be allowed to attend with the other braves in the war party that will go to the villages of the White Man and make war?" Maxkii-Wiixcheew asked, looking up into the eyes of Standing Bear, whose smile faded from his face.

"No, my brother, you cannot come with us."

"Am I not big enough to fight? Or at least carry your weapons?"

Standing Bear stepped back for a moment in mock contemplation, as if to size up the young boy there before him – a young boy with such an earnest expression on his face, hanging on his every word.

"You are plenty big enough, plus you have the twin wolves at your beck and call to lend assistance in the coming battles to be waged," he said, motioning to his faithful companions.

They sat erect and at attention, their heads in that telltale tilt position of theirs. They seemed to know they were the topic of the conversation. "That is why your job – and theirs – is to guard our rear flank, so to speak.

"You must stay behind with the villagers to protect them in case the White Man comes again to finish them off. Lead them in our absence. If the Whites come for them, take them into the forest to hide until the danger passes. That is your job. It is a very important one. We do not want the war party to fear that their loved ones have been left behind in a vulnerable position. They must concentrate on the task at hand, secure in the knowledge that the red wolf and his two guardians are on the job, protecting their families from danger."

Typical of any other young boy hearing such words, Maxkii-Wiixcheew was neither altogether convinced of the explanation Standing Bear gave him as to why he could not join the war party, nor happy to hear that he was not big enough to go with the men on their mission.

He was, it would seem, just a boy and not yet a man.

But he nodded his head and gave a slight bow to Standing Bear before turning away and towards his home where the rest of his clan lived. The twin wolves, as always, followed him, keeping a respectful distance.

They had become part of a pack, with Maxkii-Wiixcheew as their pack leader. They assumed that the pack had expanded to include the hunting party, although the other braves with whom they traveled gave them concerned looks.

"Don't worry," Maxkii-Wiixcheew told them, "they will be good scouts and good hunters for us."

In the days that followed the massacre and hostage-taking, the Esopus and their allied tribes and clans of the Hudson Valley planned their response to the outrage of the Great White Father to the east, who would not return the captive leaders of the Esopus. They were later to discover that they had been sold into slavery and sent to the island of Curacao, never to be seen again.

There were to be two war parties. One was to be sent to the village and fort known as Wiltwijck where the Dutch had settled many years previously, much to the consternation of the Esopus (once they discovered the real intent of their new neighbors).

The other was a place called Nieuwdorp that the locals referred to as the "New Village," where Huguenots from Wiltwijck had moved to set up their own community. The Esopus were not pleased with this latest development and did not give permission for the New Village to be placed on their land.

The DuBois were among the families living in Nieuwdorp.

NAALAN - The Fall of Nieuwdorp

Abraham grabbed an extra biscuit from the breakfast table, eyeing his mother to make sure he was not out of bounds.

He thought she might be too busy fussing with the infant Jacob, a recent addition to the family, to notice. "May I be excused? Father is already out in the stalls. He needs my help to get the oxen ready for the work today in the fields."

"Yes, you may be excused, young man, along with that extra biscuit. I suppose you will need a little extra meat on your bones to carry you through the hard work in store for you today," she said, her eyes still trained on little Jacob as she fussed some more with his bib. She looked up and gave Abraham that knowing smile of hers before he headed out the door.

Isaac stopped to grab another biscuit of his own before following after his brother. He glanced up at his mother.

She smiled her approval, and then shook her head as the door slammed behind the two boys running out to see what their father had been up to.

Step was already yoked and just about ready to pull the plow out to the fields, with Louis DuBois at the helm. The morning sun was just beginning to peek out of the low-hanging clouds off in the distance.

"Well, lads, you are both up rather early this morning."

"We are here to help you in the fields today, Father. Well, at least I am. Isaac might still be too little to be much help." Abraham jerked a thumb in the direction of his little brother, who was wearing a big frown on his face.

"I'm afraid you both will have to stay here and look after your mother and little Jacob while the menfolk are out in the fields. We have gotten word of some trouble in the offing and need to check out the woods next to the fields. I can't risk getting you two boys mixed up with problems we encounter – or getting distracted worrying that you might be in some sort of danger."

"Is it wolves?" Isaac wanted to know.

"That is part of it, from what I understand," his father told him. There was much more to it than that, but he didn't want to cause a panic and certainly did not want their mother to hear about the rumors that the Esopus were not happy with the new arrangements in the New Village. Neither he nor the other men working the field that day had an inkling that the Dutch soldiers had taken hostages – or of what was about to happen to their women and children left behind.

"Are you going to shoot them?" Isaac saw the rifle slung across his father's shoulder, his eyes widening as a look of concern spread across his face.

Louis came out from behind the plow and knelt down to eye level to the little boy. "I promise I will shoot to kill only when I absolutely must." He tousled the boy's hair with one hand, putting the other on his knee as he rose up.

Then he went back behind the plow. Isaac was satisfied with his father's answer and wandered off, plopping down in a field of grass and flowers, watching butterflies.

Isaac may have been satisfied, but Abraham was not. He stood with his arms folded across his chest, rising to what he thought was his tallest height.

His father looked at him for a moment. Step did, too.

"Your time will come. I know it can't come soon enough for you. I was the same way when I was your age. But I am not making excuses when I say you need to stay here and look after your mother and your brothers. I need for you to do that for me, son. Everyone has a job to do, and for now that is yours."

He whipped the reins and yelled "giddy-up" to the ox.

Step didn't budge.

He brandished the whip, striking the ox on the backside with a side-long blow. The ox barely twitched. He swished his tail where the lash had stung his hind quarters.

Then he turned his head back and looked at Abraham again.

Louis saw what was happening. He smiled and called out to his son. "Little man, mind helping out a little bit here?"

"STEP UP!" he called out in a clear, loud voice that was so loud he could swear he heard it echo through the valley.

The ox lurched forward, carrying Louis and the plow towards the fields. Louis had to move his legs fast to keep up, pausing just long enough to shoot an appreciative smile and look back at his son before turning around and running after the ox barrelling forward with plow, and eventually man, in tow.

The sun was high in the afternoon sky later that afternoon when Abraham saw the plumes of smoke rising up to greet it.

The smoke was coming from the direction of the fields where his father had set off to do his work earlier that day. He did not have time to wonder long about why there was smoke coming from the fields or if his father was in some sort of danger. Danger was upon him where he stood.

A scream rang out in the New Village, followed by gunshots and loud voices of men filled with fear and anger.

Smoke was now rising from the houses in the village. Abraham ran towards his own home, the words of his father to protect their family now loudly ringing in his ears.

He almost made it to the front door of the house when he felt himself being lifted up into the air by a powerful force.

A brave on horseback had scooped him up like a ragdoll.

He was carried to an area in the center of the village. Women and children from the village had been gathered there, being guarded by two braves who stood by, arms folded across their chests, bows and arrows within easy grasp.

They glared at the captives with scowls on their faces to emphasize the point that they were not to move one inch beyond the circle where the hostages had been told to stand.

Abraham was unceremoniously dumped onto the ground by the brave along with the other hostages.

He frantically scanned the crowd of some 40 or so people searching for his mother and two brothers. "Abraham!" he heard his mother shout. He saw her hand waving among the villagers assembled in the circle, Jacob in her arms.

He did not see Isaac.

Abraham ran over to his mother. He had never seen her with a look of panic on her face. She was always so calm and self-assured. For the first time he realized that she was capable of feeling fear. She was capable of showing that fear on the usually kind, yet stoic countenance she always exuded.

"Where is Isaac?" he asked of her. She could only shake her head, casting her eyes about, searching the crowd of anxious people, all wondering what the savages intended to do with them.

They had heard stories of hostages being taken, their heads shaved and faces painted in blood-red pigment.

They were afraid and it showed.

"I promised our father I would look after him. I must go find him." Abraham stalked forward and towards the edge of the circle, in the direction of their house.

He didn't get far. One of the braves stood in front of him. He did not say a word, not that the boy would have understood the language of the warrior – at least not yet.

That would come later.

But he did understand what was meant when the warrior raised his bow with the arrow cocked back on his bow-string, aiming it directly at young Abraham's forehead.

"Abraham, no!" he heard his mother cry out.

He stopped in his tracks. A voice came from behind the warrior speaking words Abraham was yet to understand. The warrior lowered his weapon and stepped aside to reveal a vision that stayed with Abraham for many years to come. Through the smoke and shouts and screams and chaos emerged a tall bear of a man he came to know as Standing Bear. He ambled confidently forward, a little white boy holding his hand.

It was Isaac.

Abraham could barely see through the tears welling up in his eyes, not from the smoke that was swirling around him but from the release of his fear and sorrow that his brother might have been slain before he had a chance to save him.

"Hi, Abraham. Do you have an Indian name yet? Mine is 'Song Whisperer.'"

"'Song Whisperer,'" Abraham murmured absent-mindedly.

"We found him in a field of grass, singing softly to the flowers," said Standing Bear in a serious tone that belied the smile on his face and twinkle in his eye.

"Uh-huh," Issac said, nodding his head. "I was talking to the butterflies. They were afraid. There was too much noise and smoke. They like it when I talk to them."

Isaac turned to his brother. His mother was running up to him, still clutching Jacob. Without thinking, she handed Jacob off to Abraham, who very nearly dropped him.

Falling to her knees she gave Isaac a big bear of a hug, holding him tight to her bosom. "Thank God you're alive! I thought the savages had . . ."

She looked up at Standing Bear who now had a frown on his face. He had heard this word "savages" but was not sure what it meant. He knew it was not a compliment.

"They are not savages," Isaac told his mother.
"They are our new friends."

~ 26 ~

NGWUTAASH - Wolf Pact

Maxkii-Wiixcheew had been walking a trail with his two companions close by. They were scouting the area around the fort where they had taken up residence after the 13 Moons Massacre. A brave ran up to them while they were studying markings on a tree.

The boy felt the markings.

The wolves sniffed.

"New guests have arrived," said the brave breathlessly.

"How many?"

"More than 13, less than three times as many. Some of the boys have been assigned to your Wolf Clan. You are in charge of them."

"Maybe we should just feed them to the wolves instead," said Maxkii-Wiixcheew, turning to the twins. "You two hungry?"

His question was greeted by the usual duo of tilted heads.

Back at the fort Maxkii-Wiixcheew was ushered over to the quarters that had been assigned to the Wolf Clan of his tribe that were now living at the fort. He longed to return to his own village and the woods he and his two companions so dearly loved. That was not to be in these dangerous times.

The Whites were sure to come looking for them once they realized the Esopus would not be cowed so easily.

Abraham and Isaac were among the huddled children in the room. They sat with glum expressions on their faces. Except

Isaac, of course. He sat fingering a string of wampum he had finagled, already sporting a colorful headband.

Abraham sprung to his feet and approached Maxkii-Wiixcheew when he entered the room.

"Where is my baby brother? I promised my father I would look after him."

"You are fortunate," replied Maxkii-Wiixcheew. "Your father is still among the living. Some have lost theirs in this war of yours."

"It's not *our* war." Abraham had not yet been told about what the Dutch had done to the Esopus people. "We were peacefully living on our land when your people attacked us, burning our homes and killing our fathers."

"This land you say is yours is not. It belongs to all things that the Great Spirit allows to live and flourish on the land," said Standing Bear, who had walked into the room.

He spoke in words Abraham, who had yet to learn the language of the Esopus, could understand. Maxkii-Wiixcheew knew some of the words spoken by the Whites, but his vocabulary was still developing. He was hopeful that both people would learn about each other's words so they could better understand one another.

"Our way is that infants must stay with their mothers until weaned," Maxkii-Wiixcheew said haltingly, mixing both Esopus and the words spoken by the Whites.

"What is your brother's name?"

"My name is Song Whisperer." The words were spoken in the Esopus language and came from Isaac, still seated and playing with the wampum.

"He is already becoming one of us," said Standing Bear, smiling down at Isaac. "You see," he continued, turning to Abraham, "we mean you no harm. You are free to stay here among us for as long as you would like. Maybe learn our ways and our language, and even become one with our people. If you wish to return to your own village, you are free to do that as well. All we ask in return is that you return to us our chiefs and shamans that have been enslaved by your Dutch masters."

Abraham was flabbergasted. His people were Huguenots from France that had fled persecution and were invited by the Dutch to seek refuge in the Hudson Valley thousands of miles and an ocean away from their real "village." They did not think of their Dutch benefactors as their masters.

He thought they were their friends.

"Please make yourselves at home as much as you can," said Standing Bear. "This is not what you are used to, but you may find it to your liking." He looked down at Isaac. Isaac looked at him with a grin, nodding his head.

Maxkii-Wiixcheew did a quick head count. There were thirteen children in all that had been assigned to the clan called Wolf. He found the number interesting. They were to become part of their clan, at least temporarily.

They ranged in age from little Song Whisperer to a young girl who looked to be a little older than him. For some reason his gaze lingered on her a little longer than the others. Her gaze met his. He became self-conscious and looked away when the assembled children were asked to go outside and meet with adults from the tribe to have their tasks assigned to them.

Everyone who was old enough was assigned jobs to do in the village both inside and outside the walls of the fort. Abraham was allowed to go with Maxkii-Wiixcheew on scouting missions.

On their first mission together, he balked at the edge of the clearing before going into the woods. He could not help but remember the time his father had shot the young wolf on the edge of their field. Now here he was, traipsing off into the woods with a boy named after a wolf with two real ones following them.

"Is something wrong?" Maxkii-Wiixcheew asked, using his own language. He followed Abraham's eyes that remained fixed on the two wolves. "Oh, them. They pose no danger to you – as long as you behave yourself."

"But aren't you afraid? They might eat you."

Maxkii-Wiixcheew threw back his head, roaring in laughter. Abraham did not see what was so funny.

"They will not eat us. They are our brothers," Maxkii-Wiixcheew said.

The two boys had walked through the trails in the forest for some time. Maxkii-Wiixcheew would point out animals and things in the forest, telling Abraham the word his people used for them. Abraham did likewise.

They were beginning to understand one another.

They came upon an out-cropping of rock. Maxkii-Wiixcheew perched himself near the apex of the rock. Abraham took a seat on another rock just below him. The twins took up strategic positions at the perimeter, as if to guard the two boys.

"I want to ask you something," Maxkii-Wiixcheew started to say. "What are the clans of your people of the land of 'Who-Go-Know'? We have clans among our people and among those who live beyond our hunting grounds. Our clans bear the name we have in our language for Wolf, Turtle and Turkey. What are yours?"

Abraham thought on this for a moment before answering.

"Our families are not part of a clan in the same way that your people are. We believe in the 12 tribes of Israel, who are the people chosen by God to create a great nation beholden to Him. Each of the 12 tribes began with a great leader who was the descendant of the chosen one – the one chosen by God to lead them to a promised land of freedom and richness.

"The name of the chosen one was Abraham. I was named after this chosen one." He stopped for a moment and looked up at his new friend. "I don't feel like I was chosen for anything important."

"Were you not given this name after your vision quest?"

"'Vision quest'? I do not know what that is."

"Among our people, a young brave is sent out into the wilderness on a vision quest. He describes the visions he encounters to a wise man from the village who explains to the brave what his vision means and gives to that brave a name to guide him in fulfilling the prophecy given to him by his visions."

"What did your visions mean?"

"I do not understand them, but as with you, I have been chosen for an important destiny that will help my people live through troubles. I wish I knew better what that means. Perhaps in time and with more years I will."

"What are their names?" Abraham asked, pointing at the wolves.

"He is known as 'wolf.' She is known as 'wolf.'"

Abraham thought back to what his father had told him about not giving pet names to animals. He was beginning to think maybe the reason was because they could not tell their masters about their visions.

"I have an ox who listens to me, but he does not have a real name either."

"Your ox is not from the forest. Creatures from the forest do not need to be called by name by a man. They do not belong to a man or to anyone other than the Great Spirit. All things are part of one thing but do not belong to any one thing. This is how it was explained to me by the medicine man who gave me my name."

"Would he give me a new name if I also had a vision quest?"

"He would, but he cannot."

"Why not? Is it because I am not part of your tribe?"

Maxkii-Wiixcheew looked away for a moment before answering. He did not want his new friend to see the anguished look on his face, much less the tears that were trying to flow from his eyes. He gulped before continuing, looking off into the valley with a distant stare. "He was one of the thirteen moons taken by the Dutch. They will not give him back to us. We hoped that they would return him and the others if we were to offer to return you and your families back to your village.

"Not that we do not want you to stay," he continued, now looking at Abraham with a broad smile. "You Whites are not so much unlike our people."

Abraham stood up tall and straight, extending his hand to his friend. Maxkii-Wiixcheew looked at it with a look of puzzlement.

"I promise that when I return to my people I will tell them to return the medicine man, and the others, to you and to their Wolf Clan, or whatever clan to which they belong, so that you can be together again."

The twins got up from their seated positions, looking at the boy with the outstretched hand, tilting their heads in the usual fashion. "That goes for them, too," he added, nodding his head in their direction.

Maxkii-Wiixcheew extended his hand outward, just as the White boy was doing. "Why do our hands float out in the air like this?" he asked. Abraham took Maxkii-Wiixcheew's hand in both of his, bringing it up and then down in a single jerking motion.

"You think our ways are strange, but some of yours seem strange to us."

"We call it a handshake. It means that we now have made a pact."

"You mean like a pack of wolves? We already have one of those."

"Not 'pack,'" explained Abraham, using the Esopus word. He struggled to find the right one in his own language.

"A deal? An agreement?"

"Oh, you mean like a treaty."

NIISHAASH - The Fog of War

Abraham trudged along the trail, following Maxkii-Wiixcheew and the always present twins that flanked them as they made their way westward from the fort. They were one of three advanced scouting teams that were making sure the coast was clear for the multitude of people that were following them.

They had to evacuate from the place they had called home for all those months when they got the news that Captain Kregier knew where they were. He and his men were on the march.

By this time both Abraham and Isaac had become rather conversant in the language of the Esopus.

Their hosts had also picked up more than a few words spoken by them and the other captives. In fact, with each passing day the so-called captives thought of themselves more so as part of the Esopus, rather than as their prisoners.

The people that Catherine had called savages seemed much less so, even to her. In some ways she even identified with them. She saw that, like her people, the Esopus were persecuted for, if not their beliefs, certainly their way of life.

She was well aware that the people with whom she was living, with whom she broke bread, and alongside whom she toiled to make a besieged community survive did not believe in the same God that she did.

They were not, as the Huguenots back in France would say, among the people chosen by the God of Abraham to be led to the Promised Land. But they had a different view of what the Promised Land would look like, once they got there.

In fact, they did not believe land was something that could be promised to them to have. The land, and all the living creatures on it, was to be shared by all of God's creatures great and small. Now she found herself fleeing from an army of men who she should be thinking of as her rescuers.

But she wasn't.

She felt much more afraid of what they might do to her and the people with whom she and her children had been living for the past few months than she did of her so-called captors.

At this point, after all she had learned while in captivity, she was not sure who the real savages were.

They had to leave what had been the safe confines of the fort, leaving much of their belongings behind, too, not to mention the crops in the field, because the White Man was on the march, heading right for them.

They were traveling to the west, to a village that was the heartland of the Esopus people.

When they arrived, Catherine and the others came upon a peaceful village that had existed for many years, far enough away from the hordes of Dutch and other invaders from the east to remain undetected by them, safe in its obscurity.

Abraham had overheard at a fireside council that the Great White Father to the east had always intended to drive the Esopus from the lands where they had been living for centuries before the White Man came. He told the sachems as much when they came to beseech him to let the Esopus live in peace.

"Leave this place and do not look back," he told them. "This land now belongs to the Dutch."

The attack by the Esopus on Nieuwdorp and, that same day, on Wiltwijck, that was nearly burned down to the ground was just the sort of effrontery the Dutch had been waiting for.

The attacks and taking of hostages was the excuse they needed to dispatch Captain Kregier and his men to wipe out the Esopus once and for all.

Louis DuBois and the other Huguenots knew none of this when Kregier came to them to ask for their support in their war against the Esopus.

"War? What war?" he asked one of Kregier's lieutenants. "We just want our people brought home to us. We have heard that the Dutch took some of the savages hostage. Why don't we just trade some of their people for ours?"

He didn't know it was too late for that.

"We can't do that," one of Kregier's people said. "These are savages we are dealing with, remember? We will be lucky if they haven't already shaved the heads of the hostages, burned them at the stake, or God knows what else. There is only one thing that they understand: brute force."

Louis fell silent. Thoughts of what the savages may have done to Catherine and the boys were too horrible to contemplate.

He pushed those thoughts out of his mind.

"What do you need from us? How can we help?"

"That's more like it. We need horses and supplies. We may need volunteers."

"We can't do that right now," said another of the Huguenots. "If we don't bring in the harvest before the hard rains begin, we will starve to death."

"I can't give you horses, but I do have oxen," said Louis.

"You better," replied the lieutenant. "And you better get your fellow Frenchies to fall in line. It's not my wife and children whose lives hang in the balance, you know. We have to move out – sooner rather than later."

"Okay, fine," said Louis. "We will help you, but I warn you: You must be careful when you rescue the hostages. No harm must come to them."

"And I warn *you*, Monsieur Haughty Walloon. Make no mistake. This is a war, and we mean to wage war on these savages until every last one of them is wiped off the face of the earth.

"They must be punished for what they did, and we aim to make sure they know theirs was a mistake of a lifetime when they attacked our people."

"Plus, of course, you French people," another soldier allowed.

"You can call it war, but to us this is a rescue operation," said Louis. "We want our women and children back alive, with a minimum of bloodshed."

"Call it what you will, Walloon," replied the lieutenant, leaning in close, his face not more than a foot away from that of Louis. "But this is a war, plain and simple, and our men have to deal with this with that thought in mind."

"And you know what they say about the fog of war," said the other soldier. "Civilian casualties are inevitable."

With that and a sharp salute, the soldiers left.

Louis went out to the field where the oxen were grazing. Their stalls had not yet been rebuilt. The barn where they were kept at night had been burned down during the raid by the Esopus. He stood there regarding his prized possessions.

He was already having second thoughts about letting the Dutch soldiers take his animals to haul their canons, most likely to be aimed in the direction of his family.

"Well, my fine fellow, now is the time for you to show how loyal you truly are to your good friend Abraham."

Step seemed to perk up at the mention of the name. He started to move forward, thinking he had received a command.

Louis laughed.

"Well, I hope you prove to be so cooperative when you start working for the Dutch soldiers." He moved closer to the ox and whispered in his ear, mindful of the horns. "We must save the little one and bring him, his mother and his brothers back home."

Krieger and his men set out the next day for the Esopus fort, the oxen carrying their canon, while horses hired out by the settlers carried supplies. The fort was right where they were told it would be by one of the women who had escaped and made her way back to Wiltwijck. But when they got there it was deserted.

Krieger's plans to slaughter the Esopus had been thwarted, for the moment at least. They took an Esopus woman that they had found in a field of corn outside the fort.

She had lingered behind after the others had fled.

She was persuaded under threat of forfeiture of her own life to provide Kregier the details of where the last village – the heartland of the Esopus could be found.

After he and his men looted the fort and burned the cornfields, he returned to base camp to regroup and prepare for the final assault. This time Louis DuBois and some of the other Huguenots volunteered to join Kregier and his men in this last expedition deep into Esopus country.

This time they would be marching through rough terrain and rivers that the oxen could not manage. Louis had somehow convinced Kregier that he was on his side. But the words of Kregier's men were still in the back of his mind.

He knew that he had to take matters into his own hands to protect his people from Kregier and his men -- maybe even more so than from the savages.

Abraham and his mother knew nothing of these things. But they could sense the abject fear of their hosts who knew what the Kregier's of the White Man's world were capable of doing. They instinctually felt the same fear that they did.

When dusk came, they were more than eager to follow Maxkii-Wiixcheew and the other scouts into the woods where they could hide from Kregier and his men.

A new fort had yet to be built at the village. The safety offered by the forest was the only refuge they had left until the new fort was finished.

Abraham and the other children, as well as their mothers, worked side-by-side with the Esopus to help build their fort and tend to the other needs of the village.

Even little Isaac pitched in as best he could. He was not much good at lifting beams but he was adept at lifting spirits. The Huguenots had been forbidden to openly sing their hymns in public during the reign of terror back in their own homeland.

But they were now living in a free land where even their supposed captors not only allowed them to sing their psalms, but even made valiant effort to join them, mouthing words they did not understand, but could nonetheless appreciate for their beauty.

Isaac's soft voice would drift across the fields of corn tended by workers. The voice of his mother would then join him.

Soon there was a chorus of singing emanating from the village. As legends would have it, the chorus of the last of the Esopus echoed through the forest that bordered their last remaining homeland. The chorus from the forest filtered through the trees with songs for all those who were willing to receive the message of hope and of peace that they brought.

These voices of the last of the Esopus and their world reached out to all of the creatures in the forest listening to them.

But not all who heard these sounds could understand and appreciate the message the voices sought to deliver.

Kregier ordered his men to march towards the noise they were hearing.

XAASH - A Prophecy Fulfilled

Maxkii-Wiixcheew was making his way down from the mountain when he heard a fearful shriek of an Esopus woman rising up from a plain below that was all that lay between the edges of the forest where Kregier and his men were advancing and the fort being erected to protect the village.

He stood frozen for an instant of time, training his eyes in the direction of the screams he heard.

The twins stood erect and at attention, their ears standing straight up and to the sky, their eyes at first probing the forest below before training them on the leader of their pack.

He burst into a run down the mountain.

They followed.

A group of villagers going up the trail met them on the way down. They were going in the opposite direction. Among them were some of the white children that had been living among them. They had a look of stark terror on their faces.

"Stop. Go back," said the brave that was leading the villagers up the mountain. He spoke in a half-whisper just barely loud enough for everyone to hear.

"The White Devils are upon us. We only escaped when our warriors ran across the stream to attract their attention. You were wise to stay the night here in the mountain. We were not so wise.

"We listened to the man from the tribe to the south who came yesterday and told us it was safe. He said we did not need to go into the forest at night as we had been. He said the Whites would never find us, and even if they did, we would see them coming in time to escape."

"Where is he now?" Maxkii-Wiixcheew asked. The brave did not answer. He did not have to. The man from the other tribe was long gone, well before Kregier's men had crept up on the village and started their assault.

The men of the village were still working on the fort when the surprise attack came. They rushed out of the fort to grab as many weapons as they could from their huts, bullets flying. Once they reached the other side of the stream, they returned fire as best they could with what little they had.

Kregier's men chased after them.

After that, the slaughter commenced.

Maxkii-Wiixcheew knelt beside the brave, who was still catching his breath. "We must hurry!" he managed to say between gulps of air. Maxkii-Wiixcheew could hear the snarls and howling of the White Man's dogs in the distance among the sounds of gunfire and shouts of anguish.

The twins had already raced the rest of the way down the mountain to join in the battle.

Images of what he had seen after the slaughter of the 13 Moons came into his mind. He knew what was happening below and what he would find once he got there. He scanned the assembled refugees on the mountain.

"Where is Jan?" he asked no one in particular.

She was the white girl that he had grown quite fond of during her time with the Esopus. He was pretty sure that she felt the same way about him. Suddenly the idea that she would be taken away from him – or worse – entered his mind. Either way, he would lose her forever.

"Where are you going? Are you mad?" the brave called out as he watched Maxkii-Wiixcheew run down the mountain.

"You're going the wrong way!"

As he neared the edge of the forest, Maxkii-Wiixcheew heard the snap of a twig and rustling of leaves ahead. He dived into some brush at the side of the trail, crawling on his belly and then turning around so he could watch as a man, a woman and child clambered up the trail in a panic. He was about to call out to them when he heard shots fired. The man stopped, straightened and bent backwards before falling to the ground face forward, stricken by the bullet that entered his back.

The woman was felled instantly, the child lay next to her, moaning in pain.

"What do we do with this one?" the soldier said, standing over the little boy.

"He's not going to make it. Leave him to the wolves." The man standing over the body of the boy looked at the other soldier with a look of horror. "Look, these are savages. They are not much more than the animals that will soon devour them. Besides which, this boy will just grow up to be a man. You think when that happens he will just forgive and forget? Forget it. He will come looking for revenge."

"I guess it is a moot point now," said another soldier. "He stopped breathing."

"C'mon, let's get back before there are no more injuns to kill."

Maxkii-Wiixcheew waited to make sure the soldiers had left before coming out of his hiding place. He paused for a moment to check the bodies of the three people lying there beside the trail. He recognized who they were. They were his friends and fellow villagers who he had just seen, in life, the day before. Now they lie motionless, ready to return to the earth from whence they came. He did not fully understand what the soldiers meant when they said his friends were just "animals" that deserved to be left to die and be eaten by the other animals of the forest.

Another shot rang out that reminded him that there was still danger and that his other friends, especially Jan, were in danger. He cautiously continued down the trail in the direction where the soldiers had gone, stopping to listen intently all along the way. He came to the edge of the forest and hid behind a tree, looking out over the small plain that lay between where he was hiding and the village. There were bodies strewn everywhere.

Then he saw Catherine, Abraham's mother, running towards a boy sitting on the ground. He recognized the boy as Song Whisperer. A gray mass of fur lay beside the little boy that he knew was one of the twins. Song Whisperer was lovingly stroking the head of the dead wolf, no doubt softly singing to him.

Abraham stood looking down on his little brother as their mother reached them. She was holding their baby brother tightly in her arms as she sank to her knees.

Louis DuBois came marching towards them, his rifle at his side. "Catherine, why did you run? I could have shot you!" he exclaimed. Like everyone else in the village, Catherine, who came running in from the fields where she, along with two Esopus women, had been harvesting maize, ran for cover when they heard shots being fired and people screaming in agony.

They did not know what was happening other than that their village was under attack, and they had to save their children.

Maxkii-Wiixcheew watched the family, now reunited, from behind the tree. He looked out at the spot across the stream where several bodies lay haphazardly where they had fallen.

Among them was their chief. He did not see weapons laying at the sides of the dead warriors. Soldiers were milling around, kicking at the dead bodies, their guns poised and at the ready if any of them were still alive.

Maxkii-Wiixcheew looked back over to where the DuBois family was standing. He had not seen him before but could guess that the man standing next to the three boys, their mother, and the dead wolf was the leader of their clan.

He thought for a moment how fortunate his good friend Abraham was to have a father that still walked the earth beside him, something Maxkii-Wiixcheew would no longer know.

Abraham stood straight up, scanning the tree line at the edge of the clearing. Maxkii-Wiixcheew must have been leaning too far from the tree behind which he had been hiding. He could feel the warmth of the sun upon his face. The eyes of the two boys locked upon one another. They each stood frozen in time for an instant that, to them, in that moment, seemed to last forever.

It didn't last long.

A shot rang out from across the plain. Maxkii-Wiixcheew was startled by the hunk of bark from the tree that came flying five inches from his head, the sharp edge lashing him across the cheek. He barely escaped the second shot when he dived back into the woods. He could hear the bullet whistling overhead.

He did not wait for the third shot. He scrambled back up the mountain, this time avoiding the trail and heading through thick brush to escape the men he could hear coming for him.

He could hear their guns and equipment slapping the sides of their uniforms, their panting breath almost close enough that he thought he could feel it upon the back of his neck – a neck covered in blood from the gash on his cheek.

He scrambled up the mountain as far as his exhausted body could take him before finding what he hoped would be another safe hiding place in a thicket.

It would have to do.

He could go no further. He tried to control his breath so the soldiers could not find him. He brought his panting down to a steady, slowed breath. His wound made him wince in pain, but he stayed still and quiet.

The soldiers marched past his hiding place, lingering for a moment as they looked and listened for any trace of their prey.

Maxkii-Wiixcheew was grateful that they had no native-born guide that surely would have seen the broken stems and spots of blood that he had no doubt left in his wake while frantically running through the forest to escape his would-be captors.

He lay still and quiet until the men walked away through the thick brush and eventually back down the mountain.

He continued to lay quietly in his hiding place, keeping his breath steady and shallow, his pain wrapped tightly within him. He did not dare to stir until he was sure the soldiers had left and would not be back. He must have been lying there for hours.

Images of blood upon his chest and dead wolves filled his mind. Then he felt that familiar feeling of wet sand upon his face and realized that he had been having dreams – dreams from his vision quest so many years before.

He was awakened from his dreams by one of the twins who was lapping at the wound on his face. He could make out her amber-hued eyes in the darkening forest.

She stepped back and tilted her head.

He knew now all would be well.

NOOLII - Ghost Stories
'Round a Campfire

Abraham was horrified. His eyes remained transfixed upon the spot, there, off in the distance, where his eyes met those of his best friend. He saw the bullet ricochet off the tree where he last saw his friend and another that he feared had ended his young life. He looked up at his father. Isaac was still murmuring softly in some sort of chant, stroking the fallen wolf who lay dead at his feet.

"Why are they trying to kill my friend? He's just a boy. I thought you said you only shoot to kill when you absolutely must."

"That is my rule, to be sure, but not everyone obeys it." Louis looked down at Isaac. "I would not have shot this wolf if I didn't think he was about to pounce on you. He would have torn you limb from limb before grinding them up in his teeth for his supper, and that of those other wolves I saw out there, attacking our dogs."

Isaac kept singing the haunting, chant-like melody.

"Catherine, my dear, I was so afraid you would run straight into my line of fire.

"Thank goodness you're alright. I have been praying for your safe return all these many months that you have been held prisoner with these savages." She looked up at him, barely concealing her disapproval. He detected a decided lack of enthusiasm on the part of those who had finally been rescued. He thought maybe they were wondering what took them so long. "We have been searching all over for you and, by the grace of God, finally found you here, now safe and sound."

"They are not savages, and we did not think of ourselves as prisoners. They treated us well and even offered to let us become part of their tribe," Abraham said. His father looked at him with a mixture of alarm and puzzlement.

"Here, here, enough of such talk. Your kidnappers had a need to keep their hostages safe so they could use you as bargaining chips. Do not confuse this necessity with an act of charity on their part."

He paused for a moment and motioned towards Isaac. "And what are those words he is speaking? Is the boy touched? Has he gone mad while here in captivity?"

"It's okay, Wolfie. We are safe. You don't need to protect us anymore," Isaac said. He looked up at his father. "He has returned to the spirit world."

"Spirit world? He was just an animal, he has no soul, much less a world of spirits where such a thing might reside. Same with them." Louis swept his arm and open palm in the general direction of the bodies of the slain Esopus. "They do not believe in God, and so they have no spirit to ascend to the heavens."

"So they are like the wolves and the dogs or the cattle to be led to slaughter?" Catherine had decided to finally speak up.

Abraham's ears perked up when he heard that last part.

"Where is Step? Is he all right?" He turned a look of grave concern up at his father. For the first time he realized the intended fate of his beloved ox.

Louis began to feel that if Jacob could talk, all four of them would be ganging up on him. What did those savages do to them? Were they brain-washed?

"Your friend is safe and sound, as are we all. I think we have enough fighting and talk of slaughter for one day. We need to gather ourselves up, and our things, to make ready for the long journey home. At least our family is together once again."

They headed back to the village, where Kregier's men had been looting, hauling away as much booty as they could carry. They barely had enough horses to carry the wounded much less all of the valuables they had stolen from the Esopus.

The order had been issued that they were to pack up and leave before nightfall, for fear that the Indians would return and the "battle," as they called it, would be resumed.

"What about the crops in the fields?" one of the commanders asked Kregier. "Shouldn't we burn it to keep the savages from having it?"

"We don't have time. Besides, they will be preoccupied with burying their dead. Even savages bury their dead. We will come back later and destroy their fields and every last bit of their world. Then they will get it through those thick skulls of theirs what their rightful place is – and that it isn't here," Kregier told them, nearly spitting out his orders in disgust.

He had traded the lives and hides of a handful of his men because of these savages and had had enough.

He led the caravan of his men, the freed hostages, and several Esopus they had captured eastward, back towards the fort at Wiltwijck. A half hour into the journey an old man stopped on the side of the trail. He was very weak.

He was saying something to the soldiers but they could not understand him.

"He says he is very weak and very tired." Isaac had walked up to where the soldiers were standing around the old man. "He can't go on."

They led the old man off the trail and into the forest. There he eased himself down onto a soft spot of dirt and leaves.

The soldiers gave him a tin of gruel and some water, then turned to leave. "Where are you going? You can't leave him here alone. He will die," said Isaac, tears welling up in his eyes.

"There is nothing else we can do for him. He has one foot in the grave already. You don't want to climb in there with him, do you?" one of the soldiers said.

He was a young man. He was sympathetic, but he was also right – Isaac needed to come with them.

The old man was done for.

"Do not be concerned for me, Song Whisperer," he heard the old man say. "I have seen too many moons. They now shine their light on something that I no longer wish to witness. I now yearn to go to the spirit world to join my ancestors who wait for me there. Your time is not now – go with them."

The young soldier gently took Isaac's hand in his and led him away. Isaac turned to steal one last glimpse of the old man, who had slumped down on the forest floor.

He looked back at the old man, the tin of gruel slowly slipping out of his motionless hand. This would be the last time anyone called him Song Whisperer.

The caravan came to a halt not long before nightfall.

Abraham was thankful.

His bones were weary and his spirit wrung out like a dirty washcloth. Camp was struck, the horses fed, and the people snuggled in their makeshift beds, eager for what would surely be a good night's sleep, despite the harrowing events of the day and the inevitable nightmares to come during the night.

They were all exhausted.

Tired though he was, Abraham pushed himself forward and towards the campfire he could see glowing just up ahead. The men were gathered around the fire. Some were taking inventory of the loot they had taken from the Esopus.

Shadows were cast among the trees surrounding the flickering fire, making for an eerie scene that looked to Abraham like the ghosts of the slain men, women and children of the Esopus had come back to haunt the men who had killed them.

"What's this?" One of the soldiers held up a long necklace adorned with a string of large claws from what was obviously a very large animal.

"Where'd you git that?" another asked.

"I took it off that one dead injun we left at the side of the stream. Someone said he was their chief," came the answer.

"Those are bear claws," said Isaac, using the words from the Esopus.

"Huh? What kinda' gibberish is that boy speaking?" said the soldier, still holding the bear-claw necklace up to the light. He was squinting his eyes, trying to make out the details of the claws from the dead animal he held in his hands.

"Those are bear claws," Abraham said, using words the soldiers understood.

"The Esopus believe that he who wears claws from a bear gets great strength from them and are protected by them. The claws are a special gift given only to special members of the tribe – they never trade them to people outside the tribe."

"Es-O-What? You mean those Indians we got done wiping off the face of the earth earlier today?" The soldier shook the collection of claws he was holding up for emphasis. The claws clanged together making a sound like a muted wind chime.

"Don't look like their hocus pocus worked too good for that dead Indian that I took these bear claws off of back there. You know, the one who is laying back there with that big bullet hole in his head – the one I put there?"

"The bear claws are sacred. You must respect them." Isaac was at it again, still speaking the Esopus language.

The soldiers got more agitated.

"You still talking that gibberish?" one of them said. "You better be careful. We might mistake you for an injun and put a hole in *your* head."

"Yeah, little red man, you better be real careful with all that injun talk coming out of your mouth." The guy with the bear claws stood up and walked over to where Isaac stood defiantly standing his ground. Abraham drew up beside him. "That talking of yours sounds a lot like you be sassing me, boy."

"The bear is maxkw" Isaac started to say, using the Esopus word for bear.

He didn't get to finish his sentence. The soldier slapped him across the face so hard Isaac fell to the ground. The soldier hit him with the hand in which he had been holding the bear claws, drawing blood on Isaac's cheek. Isaac looked up at the man. His eyes did not look to be filled with fear – more like hatred.

Just then, before he had time to react, Abraham saw a blur of flesh and bone from the corner of his eye, sweeping across the head of the grinning soldier, the firelight and shadows dancing across his face. With one massive stroke, the soldier was sent flying backwards and onto his back, knocking him unconscious.

Louis did not seem to notice, or to care, that the man could not hear him.

"You ever lay so much as a finger on any of my boys again, you can count on being put on your back again – except next time you will never get up." He spun around and glared at the others, a wild look in his eyes. "Anybody else here have a problem with that? Do we have an *accord*?" he said icily.

He was not asking.

The men were all standing now. Some had a stunned look on their faces.

Some didn't.

None of them backed off.

"Gee, mister *Do-boss*, he didn't mean to hit the boy so hard. He was speaking Indian, and we have all had about as much injun talk as we can stomach for one day." It was the young soldier who led Isaac away from the dying old man.

Louis' chest was still heaving, his heart still pounding beneath it.

"No one has more cause to have an issue with the savages than I do. They killed my people, burned our village, and took my wife and boys away from me."

"But I can tell you this: they did not touch one hair on the head of any of my boys, or my wife, or any of the other people they ran off with.

"That is a lot more than I can say for you."

WIIMBAT - The Couple from Marbletown

Several weeks had passed since that night Louis DuBois laid that idiot soldier low in defense of his family. He had to drive the oxen a mile or so more back to the fort, and they were stubborn as usual. Things seemed to be getting back to normal. Soon Abraham would be old enough to venture out with him to help handle these mule-headed behemoths, especially that one. He kept yelling "Step!" but it didn't seem to work as well as when Abraham did it. Maybe he wasn't holding the switch just right or was doing something else wrong with this animal of his.

If Mr. Step didn't step up soon, he would be stepping into a slaughterhouse.

Louis thought back to that night he had that run-in with the soldier that put that scar on poor little Isaac's cheek. He was pained by the fact he would be wearing that little token of his time living the life of a little red man for the rest of his days.

That night, after he had calmed down enough to get his wits about him, he saw that the soldiers were not backing down. Things looked to be one man and two little boys against a hardened group of cold-blooded killers.

The odds were not in favor of the good guys.

He decided to reason with them. He told them that it was a good thing to have someone who could speak the language of the savages. That would come in handy someday when they had a need to deal with them. He only half-believed that but was relieved to see the angry group of soldiers seemed to accept that as a reason not to really teach Louis and those two turncoat boys of his a lesson they would never forget. Besides which, that one boy had a nice big gash on his face.

That'll learn him not to go all Indian on them.

Just then Louis heard a swoosh in the air and felt a sting on his arm. He looked down and saw blood. He looked up and saw three Indians coming at him. He picked up a palisade and, with that wild look in his eyes he had become famous for, gave out his best warrior scream and started swinging. One of the Indians went flying. He landed hard on the ground. His two friends looked at him, then at the wild-eyed Walloon that was drawing that big thing back, making ready to take another swing at the two left standing. They quickly decided to help their friend up.

The three of them beat a hasty retreat back into the woods and out of sight.

Louis growled loudly at the fleeing men and let out another wild, beastly yell, something maybe a bear would say to them.

Then he dropped the palisade to the ground and plopped down on a rock. He looked down at his bleeding arm. It was a glancing blow that barely drew much blood. He had been lucky.

He looked up and saw the oxen staring at him.

Step tilted his head.

"Well, I think we have seen the last of them," he said. "You think maybe now we can get back home with no further ado?"

They did.

Louis' comment made to the oxen proved prophetic.

In the weeks and months to follow, the white settlers came to realize that the backs of the Esopus had been broken. True to his vow, Kregier returned to the last village still left standing, burning it to the ground.

He knew that any survivors of the people once known as the Esopus would be watching as he set fire to their fields of maize, their last chance at having food to eat during the approaching winter months going up in smoke.

Krieger and his men had done the same thing to every hut, village, campsite, fort, or anything else that so much as smelled of Indian that they came across in the land that had once been the hunting grounds and tilled fields of the Esopus.

He knew that they had drawn away from that last village where he had killed their chief when they heard that he was on his way there to finish them off. He knew it when he got to the village and saw the graves they had to leave unattended when they heard that Kregier and his merciless crew were on their way.

He could judge how much time had passed since they fled into the woods by the state of the dead Indians whose corpses had been dug up and half eaten by the wolves.

They had an assist from the mass of crows congregating at the gravesites, literally picking at the bones of the dead.

They pecked and picked rotting flesh from the remains as quickly as they could before another set of wolves chased them away so they could feast themselves on the carcasses of those clansmen who bore their name.

"What shall we do now? Surely we will starve!" one of the Esopus hiding in the woods shouted down to Kregier's men while they went about their dirty work.

"We told you this land now belongs to us!" Kregier bellowed. "You had your chance to leave peacefully, but you had too much pride. Now look what has become of you:

"Dead meat left for the crows to feast upon!"

In the months and years to follow, what was left of the Esopus people scattered, living among the other tribes in those parts of the Hudson Valley where the White Man would deign to allow them to live.

Fewer and fewer of them had occasion to deal with the Whites. Mostly this happened when wolf carcasses were presented to the White settlers so that people such as the Esopus could collect bounties on their hides.

All but a handful of the White women and children that had come to live among the Esopus came home. The Great White Father made a trade of hostages.

He would release Esopus women and children captured in the raids against their village in exchange for the return of the White people who were still living among the Red ones.

Abraham grew to be a leader in the White Man's world. So did Isaac, although he still spoke the Esopus language every chance he could, up until the day there was no one left but him who could speak it. Sometimes he could be seen wearing a colorful headband or a necklace made of bear claws.

He always wore that scar on his cheek.

Isaac convinced the widow of the soldier who gave him his scar to sell the bear claw necklace to him.

She was very happy to oblige. Issac had a sense that she bore a few scars of her own at the hands of that man. She did not understand why that necklace was so important to him.

Had he found any Esopus left alive, he would have gladly surrendered it to them.

Not too many years had passed after that day Abraham's father came to the fort with the oxen, bearing the last wounds inflicted by the Esopus upon the White Man, that he learned why his father warned him not to get too close to beasts of burden.

He had to look into the eyes of his good friend with vision blurred by tears as he told him to "Step, Up!" for the very last time. He hoped that the end would come quickly and mercifully.

At the trading post one day, many years later, Abraham and Isaac were browsing through the merchandise. Isaac was looking for any Indian relics he could find. He was always doing that.

Some people took to calling him "Red."

He didn't mind one bit.

An indigenous man walked in. He asked where he could collect the bounty for the two wolf carcasses he had brought with him. The two DuBois boys watched intently as he was told he could claim the bounty in cash there, but he could not trade for firewater. "Ain't allowed to do that no more," the man said.

The Indian man did not seem to understand what he was saying. Isaac approached them. "He says he can pay you for the wolves whose lives you took but he cannot sell you firewater," Isaac said, using Esopus words.

"You speak words I have not heard in many moons," said the Indian.

"Are you Esopus?" Isaac drew closer, fingering the bear claws that were hanging underneath his clothing.

"No, that tribe is long since gone from this world. And I would not kill the namesake of any clan of my people unless I absolutely had to. We must eat, and this is all we have to offer to the White Man for our daily bread."

"Well, Red, do we have a deal or not?" asked the shopkeeper, looking first at Isaac, then at the Indian, then back again. Three English soldiers stepped forward, eyeing Isaac suspiciously.

"Yes, you have a deal. Pay the man already. He knows he can't have any whiskey. He just wants to trade for food.

"Your name is 'Red'?" one of the approaching soldiers asked. "I heard you talking to that Redskin over there. You better learn to speak English. Unless, of course, you ain't English and being Red doesn't mean just your name."

He leaned in, putting his nose within five inches of Isaac's face, sniffing at him. "Why, you even stink like an injun. Men, looks like we might have a real, live, stinking injun in our midst."

"I do speak English," Isaac said, in French.

"But I prefer French."

"What did he say?" asked the soldier to no one in particular.

"He said he is French," Abraham said, using his best English.

"Well, at least he ain't Dutch," said the soldier.

"Sir, do you mind taking this outside? I have customers waiting, and we really don't need any trouble around here," said the shopkeeper. There were people starting to form a line, including a nicely-dressed couple. They stepped forward, holding their purchase of flour and other sundries.

"Excuse me," said the woman. "Are you done here? My husband and I would like to finish our business and get back home before too many more moons pass overhead and we end up dying of starvation."

Isaac noticed the reference to moons and began to wonder if she understood his conversation with the Indian.

"Thanks, Mrs. Wolfe," said the shopkeeper in a quiet voice after the soldiers had left the building.

He was relieved that she had managed to diffuse what was turning out to be a tense situation.

"Will that be all?"

"Not quite. Please add a couple more pounds of flour and sugar to the order of the nice gentleman who came asking about the bounty for his wolf skins," she replied.

"Do you want to buy them from him? I am sure I can arrange a discount price and then pay you the bounty."

"That won't be necessary," her husband interjected.

"He has a thing about the killing of wild animals, especially wolves," she explained, shooting her husband a worried expression.

"You understand the language, don't you?" Isaac asked, using the language of the Esopus. He was looking intently not at the woman but at her husband.

"Why, we have no idea what you are talking about," said the woman. "Come, Red, I think we have concluded our business here."

"Your name is 'Red'?" Abraham asked. "What a coincidence. They call him 'Red,' too. And you both have scars on your cheeks. You could be brothers."

"That is quite impossible. My Red does not have a drop of French blood in him, do you, dear?"

He didn't answer.

His eyes were fixed on a spot somewhere on the floor.

"Shall we?"

The couple started heading for the door.

"Where are those two from?" Abraham asked the shopkeeper.

"Oh, they hail from a place along the Esopus River. Some people call it Marbletown. They come in here once in a blue moon. Nice couple."

Abraham stood there for a few moments more. He had a perplexed look on his face. The woman looked real familiar.

He was sure he had met the man before, but he could not quite put his finger on when and where that was.

"Wait!" Isaac was yelling after the couple who had just stepped outside. He was tearing at his shirt, flinging it open.

Buttons were flying. They fell to the floor as Isaac flew past customers coming in through the doors of the trading post.

They stood aside with a look of surprise at the young man who flew past them, shouting:

"I have something that belongs to you!"

About the Author

B Shawn Clark is an author and amateur poet who works inside a secluded "Man Cave" along Gottfried Creek in the sleepy seaside town of Englewood, Florida, where he has experienced a series of violent weather events predicted in his CLI-FI novel *20/20*.

Maxkii-Wiixcheew, The Story of Red-Wolfe, is a fictional account of an historical event taking place in 1663, known as the Second Esopus "War", when the author's ancestor, having been taken captive by a community of indigenous people known as the Esopus, learned to speak their language.

Published work by Mr. Clark:

20/20 (First Run Books), *Bricks: What Little Girls are NOT made of* (Aggregate Books); *Maxkii-Wiixcheew* (The Story of Red Wolfe)(First Run Books); Short Stories: *The Black Seed* (Mobius Boulevard), *Psalms of Hiawatha* (Academy of the Heart & Mind), *Silence of the Damned* (Piker's Press); *Look Ma – No Legs!* (Pikers Press) Non-Fiction: *How to Save the World* (in 12 Easy Steps)(Aggregate Books); Clark, B. *The New Great Replacement Theory: Using Humanitarian Law to Revive Civil Liberties in an Era of Retrenchment* (January, 2025) International Law Quarterly, volume XLI, no.1; Clark, B. *Trading Places: Realignment of Turtle Island at the Subnational Level Intermestic Diplomacy for States and First Nations in North America* (October, 2025) International Law Quarterly, volume XLI, no.3.

Learn more at www.BShawnClark.com

About the Artwork

Front cover:

Interpretation by artist SRB McKenzie of a scene from chapter 6 (Niisha – Tribe of Wolves) depicting Maxkii-Wiixcheew (Red Wolfe) in the background. The foreground image is based on Chloe, her companion of many years to whom this book is dedicated.

Back cover:

SRB McKenzie's interpretation of Abraham Dubois with his beloved Ox who was NOT named Step.

Learn more at: www.maxkii-wiixcheew.com